HOW DOES IT MOVE?
FORCES AND MOTION

HOW DO PLANETS MOVE?

JAN MADER

New York

Published in 2019 by Cavendish Square Publishing, LLC
243 5th Avenue, Suite 136, New York, NY 10016

Copyright © 2019 by Cavendish Square Publishing, LLC

First Edition

No part of this publication may be reproduced, stored in a retrieval system, or transmitted in any form or by any means— electronic, mechanical, photocopying, recording, or otherwise—without the prior permission of the copyright owner. Request for permission should be addressed to Permissions, Cavendish Square Publishing, 243 5th Avenue, Suite 136, New York, NY 10016. Tel (877) 980-4450; fax (877) 980-4454.

Website: cavendishsq.com

This publication represents the opinions and views of the author based on his or her personal experience, knowledge, and research. The information in this book serves as a general guide only. The author and publisher have used their best efforts in preparing this book and disclaim liability rising directly or indirectly from the use and application of this book.

All websites were available and accurate when this book was sent to press.

Library of Congress Cataloging-in-Publication Data

Names: Mader, Jan (Janet G), author.
Title: How do planets move? / Jan Mader.
Description: First edition. | New York : Cavendish Square Publishing, [2019] |
Series: How does it move? Forces and motion | Includes bibliographical references and index. | Audience: 2-5.
Identifiers: LCCN 2017048051 (print) | LCCN 2017059311 (ebook) |
ISBN 9781502637703 (ebook) | ISBN 9781502637673 |
ISBN 9781502637673(library bound) | ISBN 1502637677(library bound) |
ISBN 9781502637680(pbk.) | ISBN 1502637685(pbk.) | ISBN 9781502637697(6 pack) | ISBN 1502637693(6 pack)
Subjects: LCSH: Planets--Orbits--Juvenile literature.
Classification: LCC QB602 (ebook) | LCC QB602 .M333 2019 (print) | DDC 523.4--dc23
LC record available at https://lccn.loc.gov/2017048051

Editorial Director: David McNamara
Editor: Meghan Lamb
Copy Editor: Michele Suchomel-Casey
Associate Art Director: Amy Greenan
Designer: Alan Sliwinski
Production Coordinator: Karol Szymczuk
Photo Research: J8 Media

The photographs in this book are used by permission and through the courtesy of: Cover, p. 1 Aphelleon/Shutterstock.com; Throughout book Elenamiv/Shutterstock.com; p. 4 Mujiono/Shutterstock.com; p. 6 William Radcliffe/Science Faction/Getty Images; p. 7 3Dsculptor/Shutterstock.com; p. 8 Thegoodly/RooM/Getty Images; p. 9 shironosov/iStock; p. 10 BSIP/Universal Images Group/Getty Images; p. 12 Siyavula Education/flickr.com/CC BY-SA 2.0; p. 13 MihailUlianikov/iStock/Thinkstock; p. 14 Zen Sekizawa/Taxi/Getty Images; p. 15 AE Pictures Inc./The Image Bank/Getty Images; p. 16 Mike Brinson/The Image Bank/Getty Images; p. 17 jay goebel/Alamy Stock Photo; p. 18 WP/Wikimedia Commons/File:Planets2013.svg/SS BY-SA 3.0; p. 20 Stefano Bianchetti/Corbis Historical/Getty Images; p. 22 Science & Society Picture Library/Getty Images; p. 23 Stocktrek Images/Thinkstock; p. 24 Enoch Seeman/Getty Images; p. 26 MSFC/NASA; p. 27 NASA, ESA, and J. Nichols (University of Leicester).

Printed in the United States of America

CONTENTS

1. Going Around the Sun 5
2. Keeping Earth in Orbit 11
3. A Closer Look at Space 21

How Does It Move Quiz 28

Glossary 29

Find Out More 30

Index 31

About the Author 32

Earth's Seasons

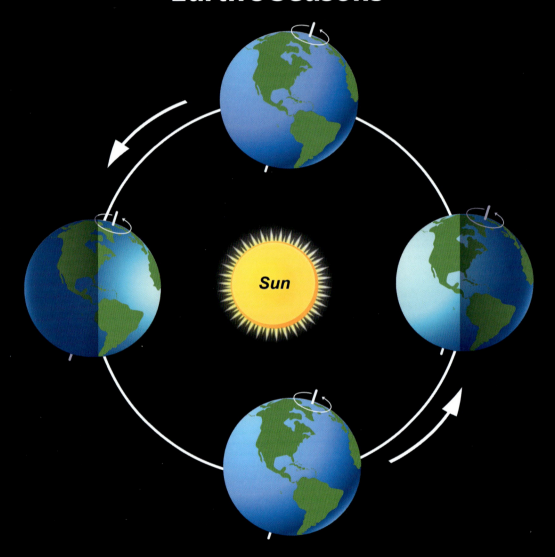

Earth spins and moves around the sun. We call this movement rotation.

CHAPTER 1

GOING AROUND THE SUN

Space is bigger than anything you can think about. Our **solar system** is one part of space. It is home to the sun and all the **planets**. The planets move around the sun. Earth is a planet. It moves around the sun. Everything in our solar system moves around the sun. We call this movement an **orbit**.

We live on Earth. Earth is big. The sun is a lot bigger. How big is Earth compared to the sun? If the sun was

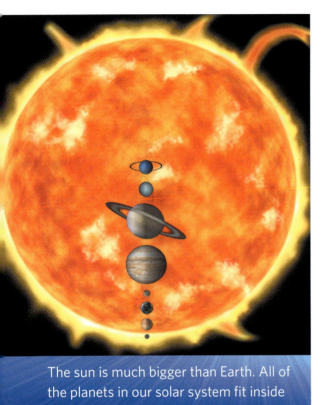

The sun is much bigger than Earth. All of the planets in our solar system fit inside the sun.

a pumpkin, Earth would be the size of a pumpkin seed. The sun is much bigger than all the planets! It is bigger than all of the planets added together.

GRAVITY AND THE SOLAR SYSTEM

Gravity is the **force** that pulls objects toward each other. Everything has gravity. Gravity gets stronger as the **mass** of an object gets bigger. Gravity gets weaker as objects move apart. The sun has most of the mass in the solar system. It has strong gravity. The sun's gravity pulls on all the planets. Why don't the planets just fall into the sun and catch on fire?

This satellite is orbiting Earth. Satellites can take photos and gather information about the weather.

All the planets are moving very fast. Earth is moving at 67,000 miles per hour (107,826 kilometers per hour). Why doesn't Earth just fly off far away from the sun?

The answer to the two questions is found in two forces. One is gravity. The other is **inertia**. Inertia is a force. It keeps objects moving in one direction at one speed. It keeps objects that aren't moving at rest. Only another force can change an object's speed and direction.

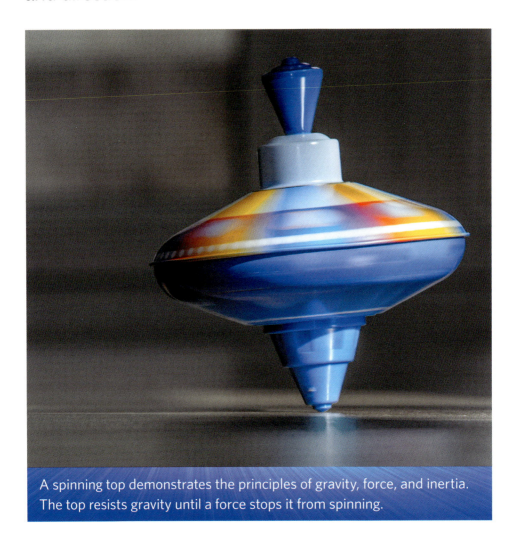

A spinning top demonstrates the principles of gravity, force, and inertia. The top resists gravity until a force stops it from spinning.

HOLD ON

It is hard to stay on a spinning merry-go-round. You have to hold on tight. The Earth is spinning at 1,000 miles per hour (1,600 km per hour). We don't have to hold on. Gravity holds us on Earth. Gravity keeps us from flying off into space!

Inertia and gravity keep the planets moving. They are almost in a tug-of-war. Inertia says move! The sun's gravity says come here. The planets stay in their orbits around the sun. The two forces are balanced.

The gravitational force of the sun keeps the planets in orbit.

CHAPTER 2

KEEPING EARTH IN ORBIT

The pull of gravity is called gravitational force. Objects with more mass have more gravitational force than objects with less mass. Mass is the amount of matter in an object. That never changes. The weight of an object changes when gravitational force changes.

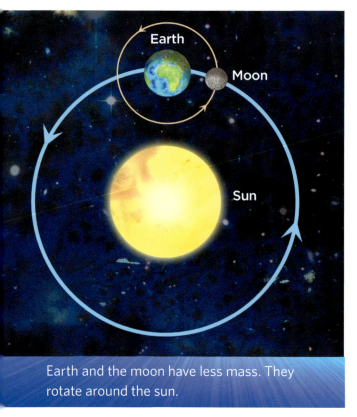
Earth and the moon have less mass. They rotate around the sun.

PLANETS AND MASS

Earth has more mass than the moon. It has a greater gravitational force. Let's say a person weighs 125 pounds (57 kilograms) on Earth. That person will weigh 20.7 pounds (9.4 kg) on the moon. The effects of gravity are lower.

The sun has the most gravitational force in our solar system. Objects with less mass always orbit around objects with more mass. Earth is big but not as big as the sun. The sun has more gravity, so it pulls Earth into orbit around it. The moon is smaller than Earth. The moon orbits Earth.

You can see gravity working every day. Earth's gravity pulls on everything. Our feet stay on the ground when we walk. An apple falls off a tree when it is ripe. Gravity pulls it straight to the ground.

Throw a ball into the air as hard as you can. It will go high. Then, it will come down to Earth. Earth's gravity pulls it back.

The big sun pulls on the planets. It plays tug-of-war with the force of inertia. Let's explore how that works.

You can see how gravity works. The girl throws her ball into the air. Gravity pulls it down.

Inertia keeps an object moving in one direction at one speed. Only another force can change an object's speed. Only another force can change an object's

KEEPING EARTH IN ORBIT   13

This rope shows us inertia. An object at rest stays at rest until force moves it.

direction. Inertia also means that an object at rest stays at rest until something moves it. When something is at rest, it isn't moving. An object at rest won't move until a force acts on it.

Think about a pet dog. Dogs are always happy when we come home. They usually run to greet us. Some little dogs even jump into our arms. The dog stops jumping when we catch it. Our bodies apply a force to the dog.

FORCE AND FRICTION IN ACTION

Put a ball on the floor. It will sit there until something happens to it. Maybe someone picks it up. Maybe you kick it. Maybe you roll it. A baby in a swing needs a push to move. The ball and the baby need a force to change their speed and direction.

Roll a ball on the floor. It rolls until something stops it. Sometimes it stops because it rolls into a wall. Sometimes it stops because of **friction**. Friction happens when one object rubs against another. Friction is a force. It works against motion. It slows things down. Friction can stop things.

This swing shows us friction. The child in the swing moves until something stops the swing.

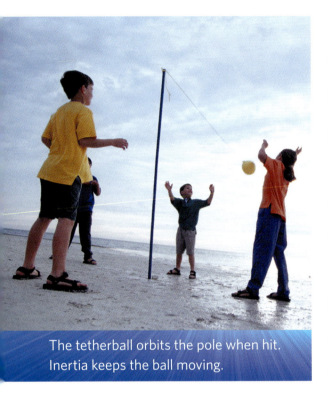

The tetherball orbits the pole when hit. Inertia keeps the ball moving.

Have you ever played tetherball? When you hit the ball hard, it swings around the pole. It orbits the pole. Inertia keeps the ball moving for awhile. If you don't hit the ball again, it will stop soon. Why? The friction of the air slows it down. Earth's gravity pulls it down. The ball stops.

Air creates friction. The friction of the air slows down airplanes. Planes need engines to keep up speed.

There is no air in **space**. In space, there is no friction. There is nothing to slow planets down. Planets never lose their speed, but they don't fly off into space. The gravitational force of the sun pulls the planets into orbit. They can orbit forever. The sun's gravity holds them in

YOUR OWN SOLAR SYSTEM

Here is a way to learn about gravity and inertia. Attach an object to a string. Twirl it over your head. When you make it go fast it will orbit your hand. Your hand is the sun. The string will act like gravity. The object will want to go in one direction. The object is Earth. It will pull the string tight. That is inertia. Now let the string go. You just turned off gravity. The object will fly off straight because of inertia. There is no force changing its direction. The sun's gravitational force is never turned off. It keeps Earth in orbit.

Learning about gravity and inertia can be fun when you do experiments!

FAST FACT

Friction makes heat! If you are cold, rub your hands together. Your hands will start to get warm. The friction you make will warm your hands!

orbit. If there was friction in space, the planets would slow down. They would fall into the sun.

The sun has gravity that changes the direction of the planets. The planets keep their speed. The speed keeps planets from falling into the sun.

The sun is the center of the solar system. Gravity and inertia keep the planets in orbit around the sun.

Some planets have moons. Moons are smaller than planets. Earth has one moon. The planet Mars has two moons. Did you know that Jupiter has the most moons? It has sixty-seven known moons! Uranus has twenty-seven moons. Neptune has fourteen moons. All of these moons are much smaller than their planets. They orbit around their planets.

The huge sun is the center of the solar system. The planets orbit around the sun. The moons orbit around their planets. Gravity and inertia keep them moving. The solar system goes round and round!

Early scientists like Galileo used spyglasses before the invention of telescopes.

CHAPTER 3

A CLOSER LOOK AT SPACE

Many great scientists have tried to find facts about the **universe**. A long time ago it was really hard. They did not have the tools that we have today. They could only learn about what they could see.

GALILEO'S TELESCOPE

Galileo was a scientist. He died in 1642. Galileo heard about an invention. It was called a spyglass. A spyglass made things look bigger. They looked four times bigger than they were! Spyglasses were sold as toys.

This spyglass could magnify the planets. Early scientists worked hard to learn about the solar system.

Galileo knew he could do better. He made a stronger spyglass. It could make things look ten times bigger. Galileo sold his spyglass to the navy in Venice. That is a city in Italy. The navy could see ships at sea. The navy saw ships hours before anyone on shore did.

Galileo worked constantly. When he wasn't looking into the sky, he was making pictures or diagrams of what he saw.

Galileo kept working. He made another spyglass. People called it a **telescope**. It was so strong! It made objects look thirty times bigger.

IDEA OF GRAVITY

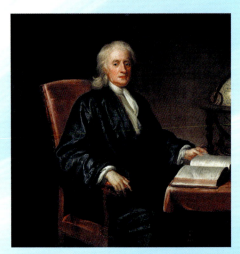

Sir Isaac Newton pioneered the scientific study of movement.

Sir Isaac Newton was an important scientist. He lived right after Galileo. Newton was like a detective. He studied nature all the time. He studied light. He invented a better telescope. One day he sat in a garden. He saw an apple fall off a tree. He wondered why the apple fell straight down. Why did it fall toward the center of Earth? Why not sideways? He guessed that matter draws things to it. The idea of gravity came into his mind. Newton then used math to prove gravity was real. Sir Isaac Newton proved the law of gravity. He wrote a book about how things move. The book is one of the most important science books ever.

Galileo's telescope let him see the planets close up. He saw that they circled the sun. Every night Galileo drew pictures. He drew what he saw. He saw that the planets moved.

Galileo proved that the planets orbit the sun! He discovered moons orbiting Jupiter. Galileo loved science. He used it to learn about our universe. Other people had only guessed. They didn't have all the facts.

Today, we know a lot about how the planets move. **Astronauts** travel in space. They learn new things every day. Astronauts can be scientists. They explore space. Some astronauts live in a space station. It is called

FAST FACT

Astronaut Alan Shepard took a golf club and ball to the moon. He is the first person to play golf in another world. The moon's gravity is weak. It took a long time to pull the ball down. The ball flew as far as 2.5 miles (4 km).

The International Space Station orbits Earth. It is like a science laboratory. Astronauts work and live on the Space Station.

the International Space Station. The space station orbits Earth.

Telescopes aren't just on Earth anymore. Hubble is a space telescope. It orbits Earth. It has lots of cameras.

Hubble sends us pictures from space. Hubble can see farther than telescopes on Earth.

Hubble gets its power from the sun. That is called **solar power**. Look how far we have come. First, we studied the planets using only our eyes. Then, we looked at the planets with spyglasses. Next, we used telescopes. Today, we have people and telescopes in space.

Space telescopes take clearer pictures than telescopes on Earth.

HOW DOES IT MOVE QUIZ

1. Which one is bigger, Earth or the sun?

2. What holds the planets in orbit?

3. What did Galileo prove?

1. The sun.
2. Gravity.
3. Galileo proved that the planets orbit the sun.

GLOSSARY

astronaut A person who travels in a spacecraft into outer space.

force The strength of an action or movement.

friction Force between two things that rub against each other.

gravity Force that makes objects move toward each other's centers.

inertia Force that keeps unmoving objects still and keeps moving objects going in the same direction.

mass Material that causes an object to have weight.

orbit The path an object follows as it flies around a larger object.

planet A large natural body that orbits a star. The sun is a star.

solar power The power from the sun's energy.

solar system The planets and moons that move around our sun.

space The region beyond Earth's atmosphere.

telescope A device that makes faraway things appear closer.

universe All the matter in space, including stars and planets.

FIND OUT MORE

BOOKS

Christensen, Bonnie. I Galileo. New York: Knopf Books for Young Readers, 2012.

Stott, Carole. Planets (Eyewitness Books). London, UK: Dorling Kindersley Limited, 2017

WEBSITES

NASA Space Place

https://spaceplace.nasa.gov/menu/play

This website has lots of fun games for kids to play while they explore the solar system.

Space Simulation Games

http://spacesimulationgames.net

Kids will learn facts about the solar system and how the planets move while playing space simulator games.

INDEX

Page numbers in **boldface** are illustrations.

astronauts, 25
Earth, **4**, 5–7, **6**, **7**, 9, **10**, 12–13, **12**, 16–17, 19, 24, 26–27
force, 6–9, 11, 13–15
friction, 15–18
Galileo, **20**, 22–25
gravitational force, 11–12, 16–17
gravity, 6–7, 9, 11–13, 16–19, 24–25
Hubble telescope, 26–27
inertia, 7–9, 13–14, 16–17, 19
International Space Station, 26, **26**
mass, 6, 11–12

matter, 11, 24
moon, 12, **12**, 19, 25
Newton, Sir Isaac, 24, **24**
orbit, **4**, 5, 9, 12, 16–19, 25–26
planets, 5–6, **6**, 9, **10**, 16–19, 25
satellite, **7**
Shepard, Alan, 25
solar power, 27
solar system, 5, 12, 19
space, 5, 16–18, 25, 27
speed, 13, 15–18
spyglass, **20**, 22–23, **22**, 27
sun, **4**, 5–7, **6**, 9, **10**, 12–13, **12**, 16–19, 25, 27
telescope, 23–27
universe, 21, 25

INDEX 31

ABOUT THE AUTHOR

Jan Mader has written many books for children. Her books can be found in classrooms and libraries around the world. Jan and her husband live in Columbus, Ohio, with their dogs Sammy, Charlie, and Annabelle.